CUPID'S KISS

Anna Ceguerra

Published by A Whim Away PTY LTD

a-whim-away.com

Cover artwork credit: Clker-Free-Vector-Images from pixabay.com

Cover credit: Andrew Akratos, OMNE.

Author portrait credit: The University of Sydney / Louise Cooper.

A catalogue record for this
book is available from the
National Library of Australia

This book is available in print, audio and ebook formats.

ISBN-13 (print): 978-0-6454823-3-1

To mum.

Acknowledgements

Thank you to Adam Guetti and Edward Pugh for guiding me on my writing journey. Your words of wisdom cannot be underestimated. I also wanted to thank the Inner West Write Club, led by Maria Issaris Walsh and Kellie Charles, who gave me fabulous feedback and encouraged me throughout.

For publication, thanks to Andrew Akratos from OMNE who produced the ebook, audiobook, and print-on-demand covers; Bronwyn Mehan, Martin Gallagher, and Eleni Schumacher for the audiobook; and Pam Sewell for editing.

On a personal note, I would like to thank my life-long friends, Billie, Katie, Belinda and Lisa, for being there through the good times and bad. I also want to thank Tita Mia and my extended family for their encouragement, as well as Sam and Hisayo for helping me get on track.

I thank my siblings, C and R, and my dad P, for supporting me through my life's major decisions.

Finally, mum, this is for you.

CHAPTER ONE

Cupid meets Helen

Cupid couldn't remember the last time he had a second date. He couldn't figure out what he'd been doing wrong this whole time. He thought he was the perfect gentleman. He paid for his date's meal, walked her home, and kissed her gently on the lips. Never to be heard from again.

So, he focused on his biggest achievement. Cupid headed a mosquito training company, and it was the best in the world; the only one with a flawless success rate. He could skilfully engineer the mRNA within viruses to train the mosquitoes via infection, using the insect's body as the training tool.

Usually, clients sought his mosquitoes to deter people from things such as loitering around properties after dark. But today's client was different. The CEO of Clime, a multinational perfume brand, insisted on a private meeting. He was developing a new mRNA strand on the computer when she arrived.

Corporate from head to toe, the woman gracefully stepped into the foyer and caught Cupid's eye. He was dazzled; unsure if he'd seen a woman so unique. Her dark brown hair was perfectly swept up in a bun, framing her oval face. Her cheekbones were made more prominent by the tinge of blush applied to them. She was a polished vision.

He nervously flattened his wayward hair, suddenly conscious of his worn-out trousers, dirty work shoes, and too many pens in his shirt pocket. Nothing he owned would equal even her nail polish.

"Hi Cupid, my name is Helen. My assistant spoke to you over the phone last week," said Helen and held out her hand.

Cupid swallowed the lump in his throat and shook it. "Hi," he squeaked, then cleared his throat to try again. "Hi, I'm Cupid." Another strangled noise sounded when he realised his stupidity. "Oh, you already know that, sorry."

They stood eye-locked for a few seconds before Helen asked, "shall we go in?"

"Yes, of course!" Cupid flinched before taking a stride.

He opened the door to his lab and let her in.

In his realm, Cupid became professional. They toured the design studio for the mRNA and viruses, the mosquitoes' incubation area, and the lab building viruses, molecule by molecule. She shook hands with his small team of employees as he led her around.

"So, although our operation is small, we're one of the best," said Cupid, concluding his tour.

"The best. I'm aware of your skills, but I wondered if you could try something slightly different?"

"Sure, let's go into my office."

Cupid opened another door and waited for her to pass, catching strains of an alluring perfume. He shut the door behind him and rounded his desk. "Please, take a seat," he gestured at the chair opposite his desk. They both sat at the same time. "What can I do for you?"

"Clime Perfumes have been attracting couples for decades now. Our team is always on the lookout for new technologies to enhance our collection. Your mosquitoes caught our attention, and we would like to work with you to develop an exclusive product."

"Mmm-hmm," Cupid murmured, but he straightened in his seat. He didn't see how mosquitoes could improve perfume.

Helen explained her idea—or perhaps it was her team's idea—and Cupid's face lit up. "I can definitely do that. All the pieces are here," he said, and waved at the shelf behind his desk. Instead of books, he had stacks of meticulously labelled hard drives.

Helen sat back in her seat, eyes wide. "Don't you use the cloud?"

"Not for immediate access. The network bandwidth is too slow for large files. We do save copies on the cloud."

"Are they encrypted, at least?"

"Yes, I'm not stupid," said Cupid, leaning towards Helen.

She gave a tight-lipped smile. "OK, well I'll come back in a week to see your progress."

CHAPTER TWO

Cupid chats to Susan

Sitting on his couch at home, Cupid stared at his inbox. He'd swiped right countless times today, with no response. While he considered changing his photo, a ping suddenly sounded, and Cupid's latest pursuit, Susan, came online. They hadn't met in real life yet, but Cupid was trying to change that. Typing on a phone was so much slower than his computer, regardless of the tools available, like predictive text.

[Hey Susan]

[Hi]

[How did ur meeting go?]

[Not bad, I got approval to apply for a promotion!]

[Great! We should go out and celebrate!]

[Lol, there's nothing to celebrate yet. This is just like knocking on the door]

[Oh, OK. How about a coffee then?]

[Sorry I'm not ready yet, let's just chat on here for a bit]

Cupid let out a resigned sigh. This was the way their chats usually started, but at least Susan didn't ghost him the way others did. And the conversation was great after this point. Whilst Cupid was a scientist-entrepreneur, Susan worked as an admin. They couldn't be any more different, but always found something to talk about; from the weather to politics, no topic was off-limits. Except meeting in person.

After Cupid wished Susan a goodnight, Helen was once again a priority. Training the mosquitoes to make someone fall in love seemed plausible, but the idea gnawed at his ethics. It smacked of a lack of consent, and he wondered if they could use the technology in other ways; something to appease his conscience.

CHAPTER THREE

Developing the mRNA

Over the next month, Cupid and his team worked on Helen's idea. First, they calculated the protein molecule's shape on the supercomputer, then fed it into their mRNA design. Once incorporated with a virus, the mosquitoes would be infected via aerosol. The mRNA then creates proteins to evoke a specific behaviour while exposed to a desired stimulus. The mosquitoes would associate the behaviour with the stimulus, thereby training them.

The extra step Helen suggested, was to use human proteins found in saliva to design the mRNA. His research showed it wouldn't affect the mosquito, but they'd effectively become a carrier. Once the mosquito bites, the virus transmits to the human target, and the mRNA creates new proteins. This causes immediate recognition when exposed to the client's saliva, so when they kiss, the target falls in love with the client.

Cupid found the new method easy to implement, and so far, they hadn't come across any obstacles. The team worked as they normally did while Helen visited once a week. She seemed particularly invested in this work.

"Do you think it's ready for testing?" she asked, peering over his shoulder.

"Yes, I think so, though I don't have any subjects…"

"I have some ready." She reached into her handbag and handed him a small hard disc drive. "We already collected saliva samples, and I organised the folders according to the pairs. How long do you need to train the mosquitoes?"

"Oh, OK… probably a week." It was a bit of a whirlwind; everything was going so fast.

"OK, I'll bring them in around then."

CHAPTER FOUR

Testing the product

A week later, four strangers filed into the lab. They entered the chamber one by one, where Cupid's team released the respective trained mosquitoes. When they exited, Helen gave them calamine lotion to soothe the bites.

Two hours later, the first two kissed... Nothing. Which was expected, since they were the control, but the pair didn't know it. Before the second couple kissed, they looked deeply into each other's eyes, then started kissing. They fell into a deep and messy kiss, oblivious to the crowd.

Helen arched an eyebrow at Cupid. The team behind them were high-fiving each other, giving whoops of jubilation that it worked. Cupid and Helen were much more reserved.

"Nice job, Cupid."

"Thanks, Helen."

The new couple still hadn't released themselves from the lip-lock. As the team urged them out of the chamber, Helen and Cupid went into his office.

Helen shook with excitement. "So, my lawyers will talk to yours and draw up an agreement to work together from now on. I think we'll need a bigger lab and team, to commercialise it properly."

"Oh, that's great; sure beats applying for grant funding!"

"Yes, you'll be a very wealthy man. Now, there's something else I needed to ask..." Helen moved close to Cupid, and he inwardly shied under her piercing gaze. "Would you want to go on a date with me?"

Cupid's love-life flashed before his eyes; highlighting all of his failures after the first date. He didn't want this to happen with Helen. "Ah, shouldn't we keep it professional?"

Helen didn't budge from her spot, so Cupid shifted away from her. She contemplated him for a split second, then agreed. "You're right; we should keep it professional." She stepped back and Cupid released the breath he didn't know he was holding. "People are already lining up to become clients. Once the agreement is signed, I'll start sending sequences of the samples."

Cupid gulped. "Sure, can't wait..."

CHAPTER FIVE

Cupid chats to Susan

That night, Cupid idly watched TV while he browsed the updates on social media. Cats, dogs, bunnies, happy couples: none of which he had. He sighed as he logged on for the umpteenth time on the dating app, waiting. Suddenly, she was there. He counted to ten, then messaged. [Hi]

[Hi] Susan replied. [How's things?]

[Things are going well, actually!] Cupid typed, with a smile on his face.

[Finally! Great to hear you found a girlfriend lol]

Cupid frowned. He didn't expect her to say that. [No, we made a breakthrough at work. We're negotiating the contract as we speak and hopefully have paying customers coming through!]

After about a minute, Susan replied. [Oh, that's great! I'm happy for you! What did you train your mosquitoes to do that can be in such demand?]

[It's still commercial in confidence, but we'll put out a press release soon]

[Awesome!]

… Then silence for five minutes. Cupid stared at his phone screen, wondering what she was doing. He typed [So, I think we should meet up before I become famous] but hesitated to send it. Luckily, Susan saved him from embarrassing himself.

[In that case, we should celebrate! Do you want to meet up for a coffee tomorrow?]

Cupid, excited to hear this, ignored his niggling thoughts; he never had a date in broad daylight. She'd see him without the soft lighting to romanticise his acne scars. [Definitely, would love to. Where and when?]

[We can meet for elevenses at the boardwalk café]

[I'll be there]

CHAPTER SIX

Cupid meets Susan

Cupid waited outside the café, double-checking his reflection in the window. He spent too much time choosing what to wear out of all his shirts. In the end, he picked the one with the least ink-stained pocket. He only owned one pair of jeans and one pair of sneakers, so there was no choice to be made there. It was a beautiful autumn morning; the air was cool and the sun warm. He turned his face up towards the sky and closed his eyes, savouring the warmth.

"Cupid?" a woman's voice softly asked.

His breath caught as he opened his eyes and turned towards the voice. She was unique, but strangely familiar. Her dark brown hair a bit messy, the fringe framing her round face. Large, thick-framed glasses made her face seem smaller than what it was.

Her bohemian dress flowed lightly in the breeze.

"Oh," Cupid said. "Uh, hi... Susan?"

Susan nodded. "Thanks for being so patient with meeting with me."

"That's OK," Cupid replied, realising he was staring at her. He shook his head. "Sorry, I'm so rude. Can I get you a coffee?"

"Yes, I would love one, thanks," Susan smiled kindly.

They entered the café, Cupid letting her through first. Susan thanked him as she walked past, Cupid catching a whiff of a familiar perfume. As they ordered their coffees, he stood behind her to look her up and down discreetly. She was slightly overweight, but seemed strong. Her fluid motions belied a person who knew her body and how to move. Susan turned to him.

"What would you like?" she asked.

"Double shot skim latte, please," said Cupid, then changed his mind. "Actually, could you please use almond milk?"

The barista nodded. "Any sugar?"

"Uh, yes... one... no, make that two." Heat filled his

cheeks. "Actually, one should be enough."

Susan raised her eyebrows at the barista, who wrote the order on a cup.

"Do you want to sit here or outside?" Cupid asked.

"Outside would be lovely. The weather is so nice today," said Susan, and they moved to one of the sunny outdoor tables.

"I love this time of year. Autumn and spring are my favourite seasons," Cupid said.

Susan shrugged. "I like winter the best."

"Oh really? Why?" he asked.

"Because you can be as warm as you choose to be," Susan said. "Summer, you have no choice but to be hot. Autumn and spring are the transition seasons to and from winter."

"Cupid! Susan!" The barista called out when their coffees were ready.

"I'll get it," said Susan, standing before Cupid lifted his behind off the seat. He nodded and sat to watch her move between the tables. She was back in a moment with two coffees in her hands. "Here you go," she said, handing over Cupid's latte.

The conversation was awkward at first. Starting with the basics like how long they lived here, how many in their family, whether they had married before, or had any kids. Things they hadn't covered in the online chats. Meeting in person was different to chatting, it seemed.

"So, I was the younger twin by five minutes. My sister never let me forget it! Although she teased me a lot when we were younger, she became protective of me as we got older, and our parents passed away."

"I'm sorry to hear that..." Cupid began.

"Don't be. I wouldn't change my life for anything! I have good friends, a sister who loves me, and I enjoy my job. Now all I want is a house, a husband and a hound!" Susan laughed.

"What more could you ask for?" he chuckled, too. "What about kids, though?"

"I haven't decided yet. I don't think I can look after a baby on my own; I'd need help."

"You sound as if you know your limits well," Cupid said.

"Yes, I try. Speaking of limits, my time is up, I have to

meet my sister soon."

Cupid deflated. The conversation was just starting to flow. "OK, no dramas. How about we meet again soon?"

"Sure I would love that." They stood, and Cupid moved to kiss her cheek, but Susan bent to pick up her handbag from the ground, not realising Cupid's intent.

"See you on chat!" Susan said over her shoulder, walking away quickly to her next appointment.

CHAPTER SEVEN

First customer

Cupid received a small parcel by courier early Monday morning. He opened it and found a single USB thumb drive. "Must be for our first customer," he thought. He hurried into the design lab and passed it to his mRNA designer, Dave, who raised his hand for a high five. Cupid slapped it so hard the crack echoed.

"Ooh yeah, customer number one," Dave said, shaking out his hand. "When's our pay day?"

Cupid's lips twitched. "You're a shareholder, Dave; you know when payday is," he said in a deadpan tone.

"It was a rhetorical question!" They grinned at each other.

"What will you do with your money?" Cupid asked.

"I'll buy a house, then I'm going to donate to entomology research. We wouldn't be here without the studies on mosquitoes. What about you?"

"Hmm... maybe same as you. But I'd also try to find a wife and a dog to share it with." Cupid gazed wistfully at the computer screen. "So, that's the sequence for our first target?"

"Yep."

"Nice work, Dave."

"We should have the mosquitoes trained by this evening, ready to be couriered tomorrow morning."

"Great! I look forward to it," Cupid said over his shoulder as he left the room.

CHAPTER EIGHT

Clime ads

The following balmy autumn night, Cupid sat reading with his doors and windows open. The scientific paper offered a more efficient way to synthesise mRNA from a digital sequence, so he took notes, hoping to adapt it in the lab. When his phone started pinging, Cupid checked the messages and realised he had forgotten the time. He set aside his notes and turned on the TV.

There, in the prime-time slot, was a Clime Perfumes advertisement. He only caught the last part of it, the words 'Love Bites' emblazoned across the screen. Cupid looked at his messages again, and he called Dave.

"Dave, I missed the ad!" Cupid swatted at something buzzing near his ear.

"You always miss the important things! The ad was awesome, very upmarket. I think we're about to be really busy."

A different buzz flooded through him. "I was reading the Notting paper we discussed. I think we can get the same throughput in half the time..."

"Cupid, I don't think you understand; you should have seen the ad... I think we're going to need a bigger boat."

CHAPTER NINE

Perfect

After Dave's prediction, Cupid was looking to expand. The lab he found was large; at least a hundred times the size of their current facility. Helen had joined him but remained silent as Cupid quizzed the real estate agent on dimensions, soundproofing, airflow, and other technical questions.

"May I have a moment with my colleague?" Cupid asked the agent.

"Sure, I'll just be over there." He walked over to the middle of the adjacent room, out of earshot.

Helen leant in close and questioned him in a low voice. "What do you think?"

"It's perfect. No structural changes are needed, only a

few minor things, plus the fit-out."

"Great, let's take it."

Cupid shook his head at the determined woman. "You don't want to see anything else?"

"Like you said, it's perfect. Why shop around?"

Helen had a point, and the orders were coming in faster now. They needed the space, so he nodded. She motioned to the agent pretending to be listening on his phone, and he hurried over.

"We're interested. Please send me the contract as soon as possible for our lawyers to look at."

CHAPTER TEN

Fancy restaurant

Susan and Cupid were seated at dinner. Cupid noted this was their fifth date in a month, and it exhilarated him. He hadn't scared Susan off yet, but he shifted in his seat. "Sorry I'm underdressed."

"Don't worry, we both are. They're OK with it," said Susan, nodding at the waiter filling their glasses.

Cupid didn't have the vocabulary to describe this place. He looked around at the linen tablecloths, ornate settings and elegant bar. No doubt the menu would be fancy too. If he continued seeing Susan, he would have to buy nicer clothes. Cupid felt out of his depth, like he didn't belong. It was a far cry from the little restaurants he had taken her to, with their small menus but delicious food.

"So... how did you hear about this place?" Cupid

asked.

"My sister suggested it; she said it's a nice place to go on a date." Susan scanned the room and said in a conspirative whisper, "to be honest, this place is too fancy for me."

"I was just thinking that." Cupid expressed his relief, then backtracked, stammering. "N-no, I don't think this place is too fancy for you. It doesn't suit me."

Susan laughed. "It's OK, I know what you meant. Should we get out of here?"

"Yes! Let's go."

They stood suddenly from the table, and the waiter rushed to pull out their chairs, but it was too late. They were already out the door.

CHAPTER ELEVEN

Boardwalk

Cupid and Susan strolled in silence along the boardwalk, where they found a cart selling hotdogs. He bought a couple, and they bit into their food, comfortable in each other's company. The silence continued after they finished, but occasionally bumped elbows 'by accident'.

Susan broke the silence first. "How did you know you wanted to train mosquitoes?"

Cupid was so at ease, he felt he could tell her his entire life story.

"When I was a kid, I used to train cats. My parents were animal behaviourists, and they taught me. Cats were hard, but it became easy for me.

"Then, in high school, I had a series of great science

teachers who inspired me to study science at university. I discovered molecular biology is my passion, so I did a PhD in that.

"As a postdoc, I attended a conference where a visiting professor from China spoke about the potential to train animals with mRNA. When I applied for a grant to do that, I received thirty per cent less money than expected, so I changed the animal I could work with. That's how I got into training mosquitoes."

"Wow… that was a… lot… of detail…"

Cupid laughed; he hadn't stopped smiling since their escape from the restaurant. "In my line of work, everything has a lot of detail. So, what about you? What led you to admin?"

"It's just something to make a living, while I live my life," said Susan, shrugging.

He wanted more details. "And what's in your life?"

"My sister, my friends, my dreams. I like doodling, but it won't pay the rent. So, I'm doing admin."

"Fair enough." They walked on, and Cupid realised the elbow-bumping had ended, but wondered if he should initiate it again. The end of the boardwalk was approaching, where a flock of seagulls slept under the pier, sheltered from the dewy air. Susan stopped, and for a few steps Cupid continued before realising he had no companion. When he stopped, he turned around quizzically.

"What's wrong?" he asked, stepping closer to face her.

"I think it's time to head back. My feet are tired."

Cupid held his hand out, and Susan bridged the small distance. They shifted their bodies closer, Susan lifting her face while Cupid tilted his down. The waves washed themselves onto the shore, in a gentle swooshing accompaniment to the moonlight. Their lips moving closer, aching to touch.

Squaaaawk.

A seagull flew close over their heads, and both ducked before looking up. Dozens followed the sole seagull, fleeing from their resting place under the pier. Cupid and Susan's arms flew above their heads to shelter themselves from the flurry of wings, and they ran towards the pier. Out of breath, they hid under the weathered wooden beams, waiting for the birds to come back.

"What the hell was that!?" Cupid rasped, incredulous, but Susan stayed silent. When he was certain the flock wouldn't return, Cupid leant over to kiss Susan again, but the moment was gone. She placed her hand against his chest, murmured "goodnight," and left their hiding place.

Cupid closed his eyes and leant on a pylon, missing the female figure who lingered in the shadows to watch the entire exchange.

CHAPTER TWELVE

Argue

The next morning, Cupid gazed out of the window of his office. This was the most dates he'd ever been on, but that elusive first kiss bothered him. Every time they edged closer, something happened. First, a barking dog, then a clumsy cyclist. And last night…

Dave interrupted his train of thought and knocked on his open door. Cupid sighed. Another interruption. "Yes, Dave?"

"Cupid. You have to see this."

Cupid followed Dave to the infection lab, where two people bickered behind the glass wall of the room. It was two of the initial subjects from a month ago.

"Why am I looking at a couple arguing?" Cupid asked.

Dave shifted from foot to foot. "They're not just arguing. It seems they hate each other now, and they're asking to be reinfected."

"Why don't they just leave each other?"

"Apparently they married and remember how it felt before, so they want it back." Dave's leery smile was greedy. "Imagine how much money we'll make, Cupid!"

"No, that's terrible. People will suffer addiction after one kiss! We'd get a bad rep like the old tobacco companies." Cupid backed away, rubbing his forehead. "I have to call Helen. Dave, make sure those two get couples' therapy."

Dave nodded, but continued watching the couple argue.

CHAPTER THIRTEEN

Date 6

It was Cupid's and Susan's sixth date. They sat at the edge of the pier, legs dangling over the edge.

"You're quiet tonight," Susan whispered.

"Yeah, sorry; trouble at work. I may have to pull the plug on my biggest project."

"Oh no," Susan said calmly.

"I don't know what to do. I've already signed contracts with new employees, filled out the lab space, spent a small fortune. And accepted so much money from all the orders."

Susan didn't reply and Cupid sighed, resigned to the fact he'd bear this alone.

"Do you trust me?" she said, out of the blue.

"What? Of course, but what has that got to do with anything?"

Susan knelt on the pier and moved her face close to kiss him deeply. Cupid's eyes widened, then closed them when he realised what was happening. Their first kiss! When it ended, he held his eyes closed as he savoured the moment, until he heard footsteps. He opened his eyes and found Susan darting away into the dark.

"Susan, wait!" Cupid hurried to stand, but tripped and fell into the water. The cold shocked his system from its dazzled state as he swam up to take a gasp of air.

CHAPTER FOURTEEN

Dad convo

Cupid entered his apartment, kicking off the wet shoes at the door. He squelched his way to the bathroom and peeled off his clothes, desperate for a hot shower. As the soothing water dropped onto his body, he replayed the night's events over and over in his mind. A blanket of confusion covered everything. Except for the kiss. The kiss was the only thing that made sense.

Once he'd finished and dressed, Cupid selected a contact on his phone and pressed 'call'.

"Yello."

"Hi Dad, it's Cupid."

"What's wrong, son?"

"Nothing much. I may have to cancel my big contract.

The girl I'm seeing is acting weird. Oh, and I fell off the pier just then."

"The pier? Well, make sure you shower; that water has chemicals in it."

"Yes Dad, I already did."

There were a few seconds of silence. "Well, if that's all…"

"Actually, I have a question. How did you know Mum was the one?" Cupid asked.

"I still don't know."

Cupid was taken aback. "Ha-ha, very funny Dad; you've been married forty years. Seriously, when did you know?"

"I'm not joking, Cupid, I really don't know. She could leave me, or I her, anytime. Choosing to stay together— that's the main thing." Cupid waited for his dad to elaborate. "Is that all? The footy's about to start."

"Yes Dad, that's it. I love you."

"I love you too, bye." Dad hung up, leaving Cupid unsatisfied. He didn't understand the answer. Looks like he'd have to keep searching.

CHAPTER FIFTEEN

Meeting

The next morning, when Helen strutted into the room, an unexpected surge of lust drove through Cupid. She tipped her head and smirked before taking a seat at the boardroom table.

"So, how come you called an urgent meeting? Are things going that well?"

Dave's laugh hit a weird high pitch. "Well, there's good news and bad news. Good news is we can move to the new lab next month. We have a thousand orders already, and we'll fill the priority ones here." He cleared his throat and pressed the remote control he was holding for the TV.

"The bad news is this. These are the subjects a month ago, and here they are now," said Dave. He motioned to the left and right of the screen. "It appears the proteins wear off after a month. Once it does, any incompatibilities are heightened. The subjects asked for reinfection."

"How is that bad news?" Helen asked.

Cupid shifted uncomfortably in his seat, and he couldn't stop staring at Helen. "The process is showing clear signs of addiction."

"Then we change it from a one-off dose to an ongoing one; a subscription model, if you will."

Cupid's mouth fell open, but the desire to do anything Helen said, won over rational thought. "Uh, Helen, are you sure?"

Helen stood and sashayed around to Cupid's seat. She rested her behind against the table—arms crossed under her breasts—and his eyes couldn't help following the feminine curves. Her perfume clouded his senses, so his attention zeroed in on her lips set in the beautifully unique but familiar face. A primal urge to kiss her overwhelmed him, but he kept it in check. Just.

"Yes, I'm sure."

"OK, whatever you say," Cupid said.

Dave looked between Helen and Cupid, shaking his

head. "What the… Cupid, we discussed this."

"Not now, Dave." Cupid waved him away as he drowned in Helen's gaze.

CHAPTER SIXTEEN

Susan responds

"What is happening to me?" Cupid muttered to himself as he walked from the train back to his apartment. The fog muddling his brain lifted with each step he took.

Susan still hadn't returned his calls, and he wondered if she'd moved on after her kiss and run. He held off his desire to call her again, not wanting to seem clingy.

When he reached home, he spent the next couple of hours eating dinner, getting ready for bed, and counting each passing second, until he couldn't wait any longer. He reached for his phone and dialled her number.

"Hello?" she actually answered.

"Oh, hi Susan, it's Cupid."

"Hi Cupid."

"Hi…" Cupid inwardly swore. He wasn't prepared for her answering her phone. "Hey, uh, do you want to meet again?"

"Yeah, sure."

Cupid was surprised, first by the abruptness of her responses, and second, because she agreed to meet him. The two things seemed at odds with each other.

"Meet me at the fancy restaurant tomorrow. You remember the one," Susan said.

"There? Oh OK, great. You want to have dinner?"

"Yes."

"OK, see you then."

"See you."

CHAPTER SEVENTEEN

Restaurant take 2

Cupid dressed up for the date, taking time out through the day to buy a suit. It was easier than he remembered and couldn't understand why he'd resisted for so long. The last time he'd bought a suit was for his PhD graduation a decade ago. That one no longer fit, because he'd gained enough weight for it to feel too tight to eat in.

As he waited to be seated, he searched the couples having their fancy dinners. A waiter led him to a vacant table with three chairs around it.

"Uh, excuse me, I thought it was a table for two?" he asked.

"This is the table for Susan," the waiter said, before he strode away to attend to another customer.

Cupid took the seat facing the entrance. One minute became two, then became ten. He checked his watch again, wondering why Susan was late. At fifteen past the hour, he took one last drink of his water, then headed for the toilet.

He ignored the disappointment that she'd stood him up; he was amazed it had lasted this long. The three chairs were a mystery. Maybe she was introducing him to her boyfriend. Or girlfriend.

When he returned to the dining room, someone was sitting in his seat, their back to him, but he could see Susan's profile, talking to the slim person in a suit. Cupid wanted to leave undetected, but he had to pass the table to reach the exit. He aimed for the furthest wall so that Susan couldn't see him, and tried to walk naturally, hiding behind his hand.

"Cupid?"

It was Helen, and his heart sank. He didn't expect her to be here, and he uncovered his face to find her. She had taken his seat, and both she and Susan stared at him.

CHAPTER EIGHTEEN

Exposition

Susan stood to greet him, motioning towards the empty chair. "Cupid, please take a seat." His heart pounded as he joined them.

"How…" Cupid took the full glass of water at his seat and gulped it down. He felt his groin become hot as he looked at each of them. When he'd drained the glass, Cupid had gathered his thoughts to form a proper question. "How do you know each other?"

Susan took a deep breath. "We're sisters…"

"Identical twins, to be precise," Helen interjected. The waiter refilled their glasses and opened his mouth. Cupid's face must have shown his disbelief, because the waiter hurried off without a word.

"But you don't look alike!" Cupid squinted at them as

Susan dragged her fringe up and took off her glasses. "Now I see the resemblance…"

Susan waited for him to say more, but he had nothing. "That's not the only thing," Susan said.

Cupid was light-headed, reducing his voice to a whisper. "What else could there be?"

"Cupid, you were our first client." Helen gazed at him, waiting.

The insane lust became unbearable, and he closed his eyes, unable to look at them. It helped a little, and he used the opportunity to put two and two together.

When he opened them again, he focused on Susan. "You knew when you kissed me?" She nodded. "How long?"

"A long time."

"While we were dating?" Cupid asked.

Susan winced. "Before then…"

"So you targeted me in the dating app?"

"Not so fast, sailor," Helen interjected. "Susan tells me who she's dating, and she mentioned a wonderful man.

I had to find out more."

"You mean the meeting with you at the beginning was to check me out for your sister? What about the project?"

"Oh, that was a bonus."

Cupid looked incredulously at each of them. "But if I was your first client, why wait until our sixth date to kiss me?"

Susan sighed. "I wanted you to like me for me."

The lust surged. Seeing them together, his loins and his hormones were going into overdrive. Unable to separate the lust from the love, Cupid couldn't bear it and he rose to leave. He'd had enough.

"Cupid, wait," Helen said. "We know this will wear off in a month, but we haven't tested what happens with identical twins. Why don't we become the subjects?"

"What do you suggest?"

"Well," Helen said, "we should go on a retreat, get away from all the distractions, and you can choose between us."

His hormones wouldn't let him say no.

CHAPTER NINETEEN

Arriving at the retreat

Cupid drove to the address Helen had texted; a secluded house in the Southern Highlands, where rolling hills and vineyards stretched out to the horizon. The large sandstone cottage was unusual in this area. Cupid guessed it was heritage listed and expensive to maintain, but it wouldn't break Helen's bank account.

Once he'd parked, Cupid keyed in a code to open the door. Dropping his bag in the living area, he explored the house, uncertain which room to take. The bedrooms were minimalist and modern, giving large spaces for the light to move. The bathrooms were tidy, and the kitchen was full of gadgets and appliances that even he wasn't sure how to use.

"Hello!" Susan called out. Cupid followed her voice to the living area and the longing almost brought him to his knees. She'd dressed in jeans and a fluffy jumper, topped off with canvas sneakers and a dark red beanie.

"Wow… um… you look beautiful!" Cupid said.

"Oh, thank you, but I guess it's just the mosquitoes talking."

Before Cupid could respond, Helen breezed in wearing her designer clothes, handbag, and shoes. She definitely belonged in this place. "And do I look beautiful too?"

Cupid's hormones raged, first from Susan's appearance, and now Helen's. "Yes, always," he squeaked out. He cleared his throat. "So, I wasn't sure which bedrooms each person was taking…"

"You can choose; you're my guest," Helen said.

"OK, in that case I'll take the one at the back."

"But that's the smallest one! Take the master bedroom. It has a king-sized bed."

"The single bed is fine, thanks."

"OK," Helen said, and turned to her sister. "You'll have to choose another room this time."

"Oh no, I didn't mean to take your room—" Cupid was horrified.

"Don't be silly, it's OK, right, Susan?"

"Yes, that's fine," Susan mumbled.

"Good. So, we have a program of activities and we'll take turns going on dates. At the end of the week there'll be a rose giving ceremony where you choose your girlfriend."

CHAPTER TWENTY

The Bachelor

They began with Cupid wearing a rented tux, while Helen and Susan wore ballgowns flattering their curves. Used to shutting his eyes against the onslaught, Cupid waited as the camera crew fiddled around the twin women with last-minute touches of makeup. The crew would follow all week because Helen thought this would be good for future records.

"OK, I think we're ready. Everyone, just act natural."

He didn't think it was possible with cameras in his face and dressed like he was meeting the Governor General. Oh well, it's for science, he thought. His hesitation melted away when he saw the women next to him.

Such a strange phenomenon; he met Helen first, but he'd known Susan the longest. Logically—if you could call matters of the heart logical—he should be in love with Helen, but Susan was something else. She possessed an extra hidden spark, and he was determined to bring it out.

As he followed the commands of the director speaking through the earpiece, Cupid shifted into autopilot. Like his parents teaching him how to train an animal, this was all about repetition and timing. One minute, they asked him to look longingly into the vineyards, and the next he stood with his eyes closed in the middle of the room.

"Open your eyes, Cupid," the husky voice from his earpiece caressed his cochlea. He did so, and hormones coursed through his body, overwhelming him. Susan and Helen faced him, each holding a different coloured long-stemmed rose. He flushed, not surprised, to feel himself harden at dual stimuli.

Helen stepped forward. "Please accept this yellow rose as a token of my commitment to you." Cupid took the rose, and Helen returned to her place.

Susan then approached him. "Please accept this dark red rose as a token of my commitment to you." Cupid took the rose and nodded, and she also stepped back.

Cupid carefully carried the de-thorned roses and placed each in a crystal vase of water. One of the crew put a glass dome over each. The roses would only last a week before the last petal fell, which indicated he'd run out of time to decide.

CHAPTER TWENTY-ONE

Mark

That evening, the three shared dinner in the cottage, cameras watchful. Helen was the life of the party, used to entertaining other CEOs during business deals. Cupid hadn't seen this side of her: strong, ruthless, assertive, in control. Well, he had, but in a different context. She included her sister in the conversations, though, and Susan seemed content in the company.

The mosquito bite didn't seem so strong tonight; maybe the effect was wearing off, or he'd given in to their control. He mentally counted days since Susan kissed him, still unsure when he'd suffered the bite. The day he received the USB was four weeks ago, so it wasn't before then. He wondered whether the one month started at first bite or first kiss, and he hoped it disappeared before the final petal fell.

Cupid shook his hips, trying to clear the buzzing, heavy

feeling there, and Helen grinned. "What are you doing there, feeling uncomfortable are we?"

However, Susan's cheeks pinked, and he couldn't blame her. He stood and lifted his plate. "I was thinking it's my bedtime. You two enjoy the evening."

"It's OK, we'll clear up," Helen said.

Cupid was almost to his bedroom when he realised he forgot his phone. He returned to the dining room, and Susan and Helen were still there, talking with each other. They silenced, and Cupid guessed he was their discussion point.

"I forgot my phone..." Being close to both had butterflies rising in his stomach, so it wasn't getting weaker. The only difference was the relief he felt when he left them. He didn't know what to do. Either stay with them to find a new baseline or accept the slap in the face when he saw them next. He chose the latter.

"Goodnight, you two."

CHAPTER TWENTY-TWO

Date with Helen

Cupid's eyes were shut. Again. The vertigo he was experiencing overwhelmed him. He peeked through a slit between his eyelids, changed his mind, and squeezed them tighter.

"Come on, you can do it," Helen screamed into the wind. "I'll count to three. One. Two. Three!"

Cupid refused to budge. He squinted again, just to make sure he made the right decision.

"Jump!" Helen shouted another order. Cupid's legs moved unbidden, first priming the pump, then releasing the energy: jumping a foot up and forward. His legs scrambled for purchase but found nothing but air. Panic bubbled from his chest up into his throat, producing a melodious scream all the way down.

He felt the bungee cord jerk on his legs and was turned upside down before springing up again. His lungs ran out of air, and he gasped as the G-forces worked on his body. Then he was weightless once more, still upside down. He recommenced his screaming.

Eventually the springing stopped, and they dragged him back up to the top, where Helen was waiting for him. "There you go, nothing like a good fright to get the heart pumping! Let's go again!"

To his horror, Cupid agreed. Despite his mind protesting, every inch of his body said yes. The wind picked up, and he realised his crotch was cold and wet.

CHAPTER TWENTY-THREE

Date with Susan

Susan was bent over, and through his peripheral vision, Cupid appreciated her behind as she plucked a truffle from the ground. The pigs and dogs snuffled about, striving to find another treat. She dusted off the treasure and added it to her basket.

She looked inside Cupid's empty one and laughed. "I didn't expect to be winning this contest."

Cupid grinned. "You're winning fair and square."

Susan and Cupid followed the animals across the farm. They had decided on a competition: dogs versus pigs. Cupid earned the finds of the dogs and Susan the pigs'. Susan was winning ten nil.

They walked on with their baskets knocking together, comfortable in the easy silence stretching between them.

The camera crew were taking a break, declaring long ago that they had all the shots they needed.

"Helen's place is nice at this time of year. There are so many things to do. We try to get away every few months, just to escape everything and catch up."

Cupid became solemn. "How come... you're identical twins, right?" She nodded. "How did you end up so different?"

Susan sighed. "You're not the first to ask, and I've wondered many times. We have the same genes, so we should have the same drive. One of my earliest memories is of our parents telling Helen she's older, so she has to look out for me. Which is ridiculous because we're only five minutes apart. But Helen has always been there for me, and maybe that's why I never tried fighting for myself."

They walked on until a dog barked, pawing at the ground. Cupid ran over and dug with the trowel from his basket. "I think I hit the jackpot!" he crowed. He kept digging around the spot, as Susan watched over his shoulder, ooh-ing and ahh-ing.

The truffle farmer joined them but shook his head. "Nah mate, it's under a tree root; you'll never dig it out. The dogs always smell that one."

"What? No, I need to get it out."

"Many people have tried and failed."

"Oh, OK." Cupid deflated and Susan laughed.

"Come on, I'm sure you'll find another," she consoled him.

CHAPTER TWENTY-FOUR

Chosen

The last morning of the retreat, Cupid woke in his single bed. He replayed his dates with Susan and Helen the past few days, glad the decision was obvious. He needed action, so Cupid dressed to head outside.

On his way past the living room, Cupid spotted the two roses bending their heads in despair. The final few petals reminded Cupid of the inescapable march of his time here. He messaged the housekeeper, detailing his instructions for the rose ceremony that evening.

Neither Susan nor Helen would be awake yet, so he hiked up to Rosemount View for one last look before he left, unlikely to come back. Halfway through the climb, Cupid saw someone was already there. The familiar rush of hormones coursed through his body, building with each step. Finally, he reached the summit.

"You know who you're choosing, don't you?"

"Yes."

"How long have you known?"

"For a while." Cupid looked intently at her.

The woman smiled. "I tried my best, but you two have clearly chosen each other. I'll leave you together for the rest of the trip. Once you realise she's perfect for you, there's no point wasting time searching for another."

"I'll remember."

They stood there awkwardly, unable to think of what to say to each other.

"Well, goodbye then," Helen finally said. She reached towards him and hugged him tight. "Look after her well."

"I will." Cupid closed his eyes tight to minimise the effect of Helen's proximity to his body. Back at the house, the blinds twitched, and a shadow disappeared, unbeknownst to either of them.

CHAPTER TWENTY-FIVE

One

Later, Cupid sat down for the post-rose ceremony interview. He took a seat on the stool in front of the camera, eyes red and swollen.

"Tell us about your day."

"Well, uh..." Cupid looked far away. "Helen had left earlier today; we met at Rosemount View early this morning. I left instructions with the housekeeper for the rose I'd chosen and ate breakfast alone. There were no dates planned, so I waited for tonight."

"And while you were waiting, what was going through your mind?"

Cupid's eyes focused on the interviewer. "I was so excited to choose Susan. But I couldn't feel anything..."

"You mean the mosquito bite?"

"Yes, the mosquito bite wasn't affecting me because I couldn't feel her close by. And then I was just waiting, and waiting, and waiting..." He shifted in his seat. "I paced a lot, worrying. What if she was in a terrible accident? I wanted to call her, but I couldn't at the time."

"And when you did finally call?"

Cupid sighed. "She had blocked me. Both my phone number and on the dating app. I called Helen as well, but she wasn't answering either." He looked down at his lap. "I am so confused. Everything was going so well. Did you guys see anything?"

"Err, let's focus on you for now. What will you do?"

Cupid gazed off into the distance. "I guess I'll go home and live my life. I'm sure now I've met someone like her, then I'll meet someone like that again, right?"

The interviewer nodded but looked dubious.

CHAPTER TWENTY-SIX

End

Six months after the mosquito bite had worn off, Cupid took a detour on his way to work, passing by the café where he first met Susan. As he always did, he looked in to see if she was there. And, as always, she was not.

He opened the door to his office, and to his annoyance, a woman was sitting in his seat, back facing towards him. "Helen, I already asked you a hundred times not to sit in my chair. Get out!" Cupid questioned why this kept happening. Whose lab does she think this is, anyway?

"If you're sure..." a soft, familiar voice said, as the swivel chair turned around slowly.

His heart skipped a beat. "Susan... where have you been? I've been trying..."

Susan put a hand up, silencing him. "Not yet. Shall we grab a coffee?"

"Um, OK, let's get out of here."

They walked to the coffee shop Cupid had passed by earlier. "Two skim lattes, please," he ordered. The barista raised her eyebrows but wrote the order on cups. Cupid turned to Susan. "What do you want?" he asked.

"I thought you ordered for me," she said, and covered a giggle with a cough.

"Just making sure," he said. They waited by the espresso machine as they checked each other out. "You've changed a lot," Cupid said, as Susan said, "You look exactly the same." Susan beamed, but Cupid looked away.

They took their coffee to the table outside. It was the middle of summer, which he knew was not her favourite season. "Is this table OK?" He stood next to a table with two chairs under the shade of a tree. Susan nodded, then fussed with her coffee, stirring it while shifting in her seat.

"I'm sorry," Cupid started, although he wasn't sure why. He thought about it a lot over the past few months, and he must have done something terrible to make her run away.

Susan sighed. "No, I am. I misunderstood what happened on the hill before the rose ceremony. I saw you hug Helen, and I couldn't bear the rejection…"

She continued stirring the contents of her cup as Cupid remembered the hopeful morning. He was trying so hard not to ruin it, but ruin it, he did. "I'm sorry. I'd known for a while who I'd choose. Helen beat me to Rosemount View, and she had guessed, too. It seems the only one who didn't know… was you."

She kept focusing on her coffee; the liquid whirling from her stirring. "I chose you, Susan." Cupid held out his hand, palm-up, on the table. "What about you?"

Two heavy tears dropped onto the table in front of her. "You want to know what I've done the past six months? I did a semester of art school, and I'm good at it. I lived in a flat with no-one but myself to look out for me. It was the best feeling ever, to be independent like that."

Cupid's smile waned, and he pulled away his empty hand. Susan let him. "I'm sorry, Cupid. When I saw you hug Helen on the hill, I thought that was it. I said goodbye to you in my heart that morning. I can't compete with my sister. I realised only I could act in my best interest if I chose to. And after thirty-five years, I finally did."

"I don't understand. Should I wait for you? Because I can."

"No, Cupid, live your own life, don't wait for someone to live it for you." Susan bent to meet his eyes, but he'd hidden from her view with his face downcast.

Finally, he met her gaze, tears pricking his eyes. "I guess that's it, then." Cupid's voice was slightly wavering.

"Yes, you're free from the mosquito bite now, so you're not obliged to be with me."

Cupid angrily blinked the tears away. First, no second dates, then the mosquito bite, and now no Susan. "You know who I want." He looked down again; he had to put a stop to this. "And if I can't have you, then I'll have second best."

Cupid stood with a new resolve as the blood drained from Susan's face. "Helen."

The End.